MAYHEM IN MONTANA

RAMBLING RV COZY MYSTERIES, BOOK 3

PATTI BENNING

SUMMER PRESCOTT BOOKS PUBLISHING

Copyright 2022 Summer Prescott Books

All Rights Reserved. No part of this publication nor any of the information herein may be quoted from, nor reproduced, in any form, including but not limited to: printing, scanning, photocopying, or any other printed, digital, or audio formats, without prior express written consent of the copyright holder.

**This book is a work of fiction. Any similarities to persons, living or dead, places of business, or situations past or present, is completely unintentional.

CHAPTER ONE

Tulia Blake had never been further from home. Of course, that had been true with every mile she traveled over the past two weeks. After leaving Wisconsin, she explored the many lakes of Minnesota, and the wide-open spaces of North Dakota. Born and raised in Michigan, the change in terrain had been both impressive and a little bit intimidating. It drove home how big her country was, and the fact that, even after traveling for weeks, she had still only seen a small portion of it. Even after her trip around the United States was complete, she would still have only seen a fraction of the country.

Now, as she passed a sign for Billings, Montana, she reached into the cup holder and grabbed a potato chip out of the half empty bag, popping it into her mouth before crunching it. Cicero, her African Grey parrot—and her best and only companion on the trip —clung to his cage bars, staring at her intently. Careful to keep her eyes on the road, she grabbed another chip, broke off a small piece, and handed it to him. He made short work of it with his powerful beak.

"Montana," she said, talking aloud to him. It wasn't a new habit; the bird was as old as she was, and her parents had brought him home shortly after she was born. She'd been talking to him since she first learned to talk. "A real western state. I'm going to have to start listening to country music. This is it, buddy. We're more than halfway across the country. Can you believe it?"

Tulia's life had changed so quickly that sometimes she still woke up in the bed in her RV and thought she was in her apartment with Luis, her now ex-boyfriend, sleeping next to her. She'd been a waitress, something she hadn't been thrilled about considering that she was thirty and had expected to do more with her life by then, and had felt both aimless and trapped. Then she discovered that Luis was cheating on her, and things got even worse – but only for a short time.

The day after she dumped her good-for-nothing

boyfriend, she woke up to find that the winning lottery numbers from the night before matched the ticket she'd bought on her way home from work the previous afternoon. It had felt like a dream, and in some ways still did. She had more money than she knew what to do with, quite literally. She was relying on a financial advisor to keep her from making any big mistakes.

The RV had been her only big expense so far, the one over-the-top purchase she had allowed herself, and the only major purchase she'd been sure she wanted to make. She had the vague expectation that she would buy a house after completing her trip, but she hadn't thought beyond that. For all she knew, she may not even want to keep living in Michigan when she got back. Maybe she'd find another state she loved even more. Minnesota had been a close one, with its wealth of wilderness and its multitude of lakes. She'd grown up in the Great Lakes state, and knew that wherever she lived, she wanted it to be by water. But maybe she just thought that because she'd never visited a desert state, had never seen the Great Plains, or climbed a mountain.

That was what this trip was all about. It was about finding herself, finding out what she really liked and cared about, so she could do something worthwhile with her money. The temptation to buy fancy cars and go on glamorous vacations overseas was there, but even stronger was the need to make the one-time, amazing stroke of life-changing luck she'd somehow stumbled into matter. She didn't want to waste this chance that fate had given her.

"Take the next exit."

Tulia turned the RV's volume up a little bit as her GPS spoke. They were getting close to their destination. Not a campground, this time, but a big chain supermarket on the outskirts of Billings. She needed to go shopping, rather desperately. The chips were her breakfast and lunch all in one, because they were the only food she had left in the RV. She was on her last roll of toilet paper, and had two bottles of water left in the fridge.

Cicero wanted bananas again, and she wanted something that didn't come in a crinkly packet.

As the exit approached, she hit her blinker and turned off the freeway. She'd been spending most of her time camping and enjoying nature. This was the first big city she had stopped in since leaving Michigan, and she was a bit wary about taking the RV into it. Thankfully, the supermarket wasn't far off the highway. In fact, she could see it from the exit. It had ample parking, and it was on a main street, so she had plenty of room to turn in, though she did have to wait a while for a gap in the traffic big enough for both her forty-four-foot RV and the sedan that she was pulling behind it.

Instead of parking as close to the doors as she could, like she used to when her main vehicle was her car, she stuck to the outer edge of the parking lot, trying to find a place to park that was out of the way. She was about to claim a spot around the back of the building when she spotted another RV—one that made her do a double take. It looked exactly like hers. That might not have been surprising if she had bought a used one at a reasonable price, but her one big treat for herself after winning the lottery had been the RV, and she had gone all out. It was state of the art, brand-new, and ridiculously expensive.

She'd never seen another one on the road, and she *had* to park behind this one, even if just to get a picture.

She pulled along the curb behind it and took a moment to make sure that the air conditioning would remain running while she ran into the store. Taking her keys and her purse, she said a quick goodbye to Cicero, pulled a sunshade over the windows, got out, and locked the RV behind her. The air conditioning would keep the RV nice and cool while she was shopping, and the sunshades would keep people from looking in and seeing Cicero. She was always afraid that he would get stolen if she wasn't careful. A small, digital thermometer inside the RV was set up to send an alert to her phone if the temperature got too high, in the off chance the air conditioning failed.

She'd known that traveling with the parrot would present its own difficulties, but she hadn't been able to imagine leaving him behind for so long. She had done everything she could to make sure that this trip would be safe for him and had picked up a few things along the way as problems presented themselves. Thankfully, he had adjusted well to life on the road and seemed to be enjoying the trip as much as she was.

She paused a moment to step back and take a picture of both of them, already grinning as she thought about posting it to her blog. She had picked up a good number of followers over the past month and engaged with them regularly. It was something she enjoyed a lot more than she had thought she would. She knew that her readers would love this, and couldn't wait to share it with them.

At the entrance to the store, a man with short brown hair, wearing a stained, too-large camo jacket and a backward bright red baseball cap approached her. She hesitated, but didn't have it in her to push past him and just keep going.

"Excuse me, ma'am?" he said. "Do you have any spare change? I'm trying to get out to California to visit my brother, and anything helps."

"I'm sorry, I don't have any cash," she said, honestly. She felt a twinge of guilt as he gave a resigned nod and retreated to lean against the hard brick wall of the building. She had more than enough money in her bank account to buy a hundred men like him houses and cars. It didn't feel right to leave him with nothing.

Feeling vaguely guilty, she went inside. The store was busy, and she felt a strange rush of déjà vu as she stepped inside. It was air-conditioned, loud, and other than the unusually high number of cowboy boots and hats, it could have been any grocery store back in the Midwest. Other than fast food, it was the first chain store she had stepped into since she left.

As she walked through the store with her cart, picking up items that were both needed and not needed, she paused near the television display to watch a high-definition recording of what must have been a local rodeo.

"Maybe I'll get to see one of those," Tulia muttered as she watched. She realized she'd spoken aloud when another woman who had been watching the displays turned to look at her. She had blonde hair that was going gray and faint lines around her face. Her hazel eyes were bright, and she gave Tulia a warm smile.

"You really should. It's worth it," the woman said. "You never forget your first rodeo. That's my daughter on the screen; it's a competition she rode in last week. It's been a busy rodeo season for all of us, but she's done better than I ever hoped."

"That's really neat," Tulia said with a smile. "Do you know if there are any rodeos still going on in the area? I'll be in the state for a few days, at least."

"There are plenty throughout the summer. Even though it's getting toward the end of the season, I'm sure you'd even be able to hit more than one if you're willing to drive a bit. Where are you from?"

"Michigan," Tulia said. "We have fairs and stuff, but no real rodeos."

"Well, the small, local ones can be just as fun as the big ones, especially if you're new to the circuit," the woman said. "It's worth going to one if you've got the time."

"Thanks. I'll have to look up the local rodeos later. I'm Tulia, by the way. Tulia Blake."

She shook the woman's hand. "Olivia Adkins. It's

nice to meet you. You know, you remind me of my daughter. You've got the same hair, and the same eyes."

Tulia didn't know what to say to that. The other woman looked sad at the mention of her daughter, and she wondered why. "Thanks," she settled on at last. "I'm sure your daughter is beautiful."

She winced, realizing that might sound a bit arrogant since the other woman had just compared their looks, but Olivia just laughed. "She is. She is my pride and joy. We just met for lunch, before she heads off to her next big rodeo show. I just hope she knows how proud of her I am."

"I'm sure she does," Tulia said. "I'd better get going. It really was nice to meet you."

They parted ways, Tulia pushing her cart on as she perused the aisles, trying to plan ahead so she wouldn't have to make another shopping stop for a while.

It was still strange to check out without feeling guilty about how much money she was spending, and, remembering the homeless man who had asked her for a few dollars, she hit the button to get cash back at the register. She knew she couldn't just go throwing around big amounts of money willy-nilly, not if she wanted her funds to last. Even though it seemed impossible to her, her financial advisor had impressed upon her how quickly the sixty million she had been left with after taxes could vanish if she wasn't careful, but she also didn't want to be miserly. She could afford to hand a hundred off to the man outside the store and make his day.

Walking out with her cart full of bags and the money in her hand, she looked around for the man but didn't see him anywhere. Feeling bad that she had missed him, she slipped the bill into her wallet. Maybe she'd get a chance to do her good deed for the day later. She wasn't sure how much longer she'd be in Billings, but she wasn't ready to leave the city behind quite yet.

CHAPTER TWO

Tulia made her way back to her RV and unloaded her grocery bags, then returned the cart to the nearest cart corral. Climbing up into the RV, she secured the screen door behind her, but left the main door open, wanting to get some fresh air while she unpacked and put away her food.

Cicero whistled in greeting, and she paused to scratch his head through the cage bars. "I got you some tasty snacks," she told him. "Give me a few minutes, and I'll chop up some fruit for you."

She unpacked the food at her leisure, keeping out a few grapes and a banana to make a fruit bowl for Cicero when she was done. Not being constantly in a hurry was something she was still getting used to. It felt odd—but nice—to know she didn't have to rush to be anywhere or to prepare for her shift at work. If she wanted to, she could spend all day relaxing before driving off to find a camping spot. Heck, she could probably just keep the RV here overnight—when she was doing her research before leaving for the trip, she'd learned the big supermarkets that were open all night were often friendly to people who needed a place to park for the night—but she'd rather be surrounded by nature than a bunch of asphalt.

Once she'd put all of her purchases away, she chopped up the fruit on a cutting board before scraping it into Cicero's food bowl. She kept half of the banana out for herself, and returned to the front seat to eat it, peering through the sun shade. The other RV was still parked in front of her, and she wondered who owned it. She was tempted to go out and say hi to the owner if they showed up before she was ready to leave but had a feeling that might be a bit strange.

"Kinda crazy how we're halfway across the country and this parking lot looks the exact same as any of the hundred I've been in back in Michigan," she said to Cicero, who had bits of banana and grape skin on his beak. "I guess places like this are meant to look interchangeable."

He ignored her in favor of his food, and she sighed, taking a bite of her half of the banana. Maybe she was getting just the slightest bit lonely. It had been over a month since she left her friends and family behind in Michigan, and while she had made new friends on her trip, she left them behind again just as quickly. It felt like it had been forever since she'd just gone out to get a coffee with someone, or had a friend over for a movie night.

She toyed with the idea of video calling her parents or one of her friends from back home, but in her current mood, it might just make her feel lonelier. She'd be better off focusing on the next leg of her trip and making some plans that she could look forward to.

Finishing her banana, she got up to grab her laptop and set it up on the dashboard. Propping her feet up on the passenger seat next to Cicero's strapped-in cage, she turned it on and waited for the lock screen to load. After logging in, she shared the photo of the two RVs to it from her phone, and then navigated to the blog hosting website she used. *Tulia's Travels* had changed and evolved somewhat over the weeks. At first, she had intended the blog mostly as a way to record her adventures for herself and a select few friends, but it had grown and evolved past that, with over a thousand regular readers now.

The number wasn't anything compared to the

most popular blogs, of course, but it felt huge to her. True, her trip had been a bit more … eventful than she'd expected, at least in the beginning, but she still couldn't understand why so many people were interested in what she had to say.

She wasn't about to complain, though. Leaning forward, she began to type, detailing her trip through Montana to her first stop, and describing her surprise and amusement at finding her RV's twin. Adding the picture to the post, she read it over and was about to click on the "post" button when she heard voices outside.

Looking up, she spotted two people approaching the entrance to the RV in front of her. Both people had their backs turned to her, but she recognized the man's ball cap easily. He was thc man who had asked her for money outside the store. The other person had long, blonde hair, but she couldn't tell anything about them other than that before they stepped up into their RV, the man close behind.

Jumping up, she grabbed her wallet out of her purse and fished the hundred out if it, then hesitated. Would it be weird to give it to him now? The owner of the other RV seemed to be helping him already.

Then she put her purse down firmly. Who cared if it was weird? She had the chance to help a nice man, and it wasn't like anyone here would ever see her again anyway. Embarrassing herself didn't matter; doing the right thing did.

Opening her own RV's screen door, she stepped outside. The two of them had already entered the other RV and shut the door, and she almost faltered again, but pressed on. Walking over, she raised a fist and knocked on the door, then stepped back to wait for a response.

Instead of someone pulling the door open, though, the RV's engine started. Wondering if somehow, they hadn't heard her, she knocked again just as the entire vehicle jolted as it shifted into drive.

The RV began to move and Tulia hurriedly backed away, watching as it pulled away and moved through the parking lot, heading for the exit. It was already turning onto the main road when she remembered something someone had told her weeks ago—something she had almost completely forgotten about in the time since.

A rumor, that was all. A few news articles and a blurry picture she'd seen on a website on someone's phone of a person with long, light colored hair, an RV that looked like hers, and a trail of bodies starting on the east coast and heading west.

A serial killer who targeted transient men.

She'd barely believed it despite what the private investigator, Samuel Nobel, had told her, and she still wasn't sure her mind wasn't just playing tricks on her, but the description was too close to be a coincidence. *No one* had this same model of RV. No one except for her and, apparently, the person who had just driven away with the man who might be their next victim in tow.

CHAPTER THREE

"No way," she said, staring after the RV. She had not just witnessed a kidnapping. She hadn't seen a killer drive away with their latest victim.

She returned to her own RV, climbing inside and locked the door behind her. Despite the fact that the danger, if there was any, had left, she felt unsettled. It was tempting—so tempting—to just ignore the warning bells in her mind and move on with her life. She wanted to find an RV campsite near Billings, then take her car back into the city and explore it.

But she couldn't ignore what Samuel Noble had told her. Sure, he had thought *she* was the serial killer, but he had shown her proof that someone matching the description he had given her was out there, killing people.

She couldn't just ignore that. Every second she hesitated, the other RV was getting further away.

Taking a deep breath and wondering if she would regret this later, she tossed her laptop and the sun shade onto the floor, buckled herself into the driver's seat, and started the engine. Pulling away from the curb as quickly as she dared, she made her way through the parking lot and waited to turn onto the road in the direction the RV had gone. It was already out of sight, but surely it couldn't be too hard to catch up to. She was willing to bet that whoever was behind the wheel was making a beeline for the freeway. They'd come from the east coast, so they were probably going to continue on their way west. It was a guess, but it was the best she had to go on.

Finally able to make her turn, Tulia pulled out onto the street. It was busy, and she had to drive carefully, keenly aware of how large her RV was compared to the other vehicles on the street. Even the huge pickup trucks were small compared to it.

It was just before the turn onto the freeway that she saw the sign. *Police, .5 miles.* It pointed her down a side road just before her exit, and after only a second's hesitation, she took the turn quickly enough to make the RV sway.

The police could help her. She'd been planning on

having the other RV in her sights before she called them, but the police at the station would be able to respond quickly, and would probably be able to catch up to the killer before she did.

The police station was easy to find. It had a small parking lot and not much room for her RV, but she managed to pull in and park along the back, taking up quite a few spaces but out of the way of any cars that would need to go in or out. Leaving the RV running for Cicero, she grabbed her purse and went inside.

The building was modern, with cool air-conditioning and a police receptionist who met her with a businesslike attitude.

"Good afternoon, miss. How can I help you? Do you have an appointment?"

"No. I need to report a crime," Tulia said firmly. "A kidnapping."

The receptionist leaned forward, her eyes sharpening. "When did this crime take place?"

"Just a few minutes ago." She took a deep breath. "I was walking out of the supermarket just down the road from here when I saw someone leading a man into an RV."

"Why do you believe this was a kidnapping?" The woman looked skeptical now.

"The person—the woman who was leading him

into the RV is a serial killer," Tulia said. "Look." She pulled up the same article Samuel had shown her on her phone and handed it over. The receptionist read through it, her brow creasing. After a second, her eyes flicked up to Tulia's face, then out the window to her RV. She handed the phone back.

"Is this some sort of publicity stunt? If this is a prank, you're breaking the law. We don't appreciate our time wasted."

"It's not a prank," Tulia said, taking her phone back. "This is serious. I think the guy was homeless— he asked me for money and said he was trying to hitchhike to California. She's going to kill him."

"Let me get this right," the woman said slowly. "You're reporting that a woman who matches your description, in the same RV you have, picked up a man who said he was hitchhiking and drove away with him."

Tulia hesitated. When said like that, it did sound a bit crazy. "Look, I know how it sounds—"

The receptionist sighed. "Miss, are you reporting yourself for this crime? Do you have a man in that RV you're planning on killing?"

"No, of course not, but—"

"Did this man appear to be under duress when he

got into the other person's vehicle? Did they make any threats against him?"

"No—"

"Do you have any reason at all to believe a crime occurred other than an article dated months ago from the other side of the country?"

Tulia knew her cheeks were flaming red. "No."

"Then please, leave before I press charges for wasting law enforcement's time."

Angry and embarrassed, Tulia left the police station and returned to her RV. She wanted to blame the other woman for not believing her, but if she took a second to look at it from her perspective, she could see why she didn't. Tulia looked like a crazy person. Heck, Tulia hadn't even believed Samuel herself when he first told her about her murderous doppelgänger.

She couldn't even flee from her embarrassment quickly; it took her a painfully long time to back the RV with her car attached out of the parking lot and pull onto the main road again. She took the freeway on-ramp, but didn't know if she had a hope of catching up to the other RV now.

She kept her eyes peeled as she headed west down the freeway, looking for the other RV while mentally kicking herself for stopping. If that man got killed, it would be all her fault. She shouldn't have hesitated, shouldn't have done anything but jump in her RV and follow them. She should have trusted her gut.

A couple of miles passed, and slowly, it started to sink in that she just wasn't going to catch up to the other RV. She didn't dare go more than a mile or two above the speed limit; if she lost control of her vehicle or someone stopped suddenly in front of her, she could seriously injure or hurt someone, and that was the last thing she wanted. For all she knew, the other RV was speeding along at ten or fifteen miles above the speed limit, and they already had distance on her.

If she wanted to have a hope of catching up to them, she'd have to try to figure out where they were going. She'd have to trust her gut.

And her gut said they were going to keep going west.

If only she had Samuel's number. He and his partner, Marc, had been hired by a loved one of one of the killer's victims out east, and had travelled across the country trying to track the killer down with limited information to go on. Granted, they'd found the wrong person when they decided to follow her in Michigan, but they meant well. She hadn't seen either for weeks; Marc had been shot and was in recovery, and Samuel had lost her somewhere in Minnesota. She didn't know if he was still tracking her, or if he had given up.

She wished he was here now. If anyone would know what to do in this situation, it was him. She'd finally found the killer he was after, and for all she knew, he was back on the other side of the country, having given up for good.

CHAPTER FOUR

The freeway led her southwest, then west, through the rimrocks and past various small towns, any one of which could have been the killer's destination. Tulia felt more and more hopeless as she continued to drive. Montana was a big state, with lots of places for someone to disappear, even if they were in a fancy RV.

Finally, she had to stop for gas. She took an exit near a town called Columbus. It couldn't have been more different than Columbus, Ohio. It was tiny, but gorgeous, with mountains visible in the distance. It was the sort of place she might want to stay for a night or two normally, but even though she knew she wouldn't be able to catch up to the other RV, she couldn't stomach the thought of just giving up.

Pulling up to a gas station that offered diesel, she got out and went inside to pay, intending to grab a cold drink while she was at it. After selecting a soda, she went up to the counter, where an elderly man was staring out the window at her RV. He turned to her when she put her drink down.

"Now, I might be old, but I ain't crazy yet," he said. "Didn't I just sell you gas not even an hour ago?"

She blinked, not believing it at first, then felt a rush go through her. Leaning forward with her hands on the counter, she said, "Did another person with the same RV come through here?"

"'Bout an hour ago, like I said," he told her, ringing the drink up. "How much do you want on the pump?"

She said a number, knowing it wouldn't fill her up but would give her enough fuel to drive for another couple hours. While he typed up her total, she wracked her mind. There was no way. But ... this was the first exit she'd seen in a while that advertised diesel. It was secluded, small, not somewhere one was likely to run into the police. It was *possible.*

"Can you tell me where the other RV went?" Tulia asked, handing over her card.

"You sure that wasn't you?" he asked doubtfully.

"You didn't come in, but I saw ya' through the window. Blonde hair, same vehicle. I guess you didn't have the car on the back then…"

"It wasn't me," she said, trying to keep calm. "Can you please just tell me the direction they went? Did they get back on the freeway?"

"I can't say that they did," he said, sliding her card through the machine and then handing it back to her. "Looked to me like they went the opposite direction. They went right out of the parking lot, and it looked like they were getting ready to turn left at the next road. It's an old dirt road that leads out to state land. They friends of yours?"

"Not exactly," Tulia said, turning to go. "Have a nice day."

"Good luck with whatever it is you're doing!" he called after her as she left.

Tulia had never been so frustrated waiting for gas to pump. The numbers seemed to tick up agonizingly slowly, with every second another moment that the other RV was getting farther away. She couldn't believe her luck; she just hoped it was enough. She wanted to save that man.

Finally, the pump clicked off, and she replaced the nozzle, sealed her fuel tank, and got back into the vehicle. Cicero whistled, then said, "Whatcha doin'?" as she started the engine.

"Sorry, bud," she said as she pulled away from the pump and turned right down the road. "I know today's been super boring, but this is important."

African greys were extremely smart, one of the smartest animals in the world, but she knew he wouldn't understand if she explained that she was trying to stop a murder from taking place. All he was aware of was that they had been having a nice, relaxing meal together, she had finally stopped driving and started paying attention to him again, then in the blink of an eye everything changed, and she had turned into a tense mess who couldn't look away from the road.

She would make it up to him, but it would have to wait. She was getting close. Hopefully, she wasn't too late.

She spotted the road the man in the gas station had mentioned almost right away. It was only a few hundred feet down from the gas station's entrance. There was a sun-worn road sign and bump as she left the asphalt and travelled onto the dirt surface. She had to go slower here; her RV might have had state of the art suspension, but that didn't mean it was designed for rough roads like this.

The road led into hilly terrain, and wound through the trees. Some of Tulia's excitement faded; if there was another turnoff, she would never be able to tell if the other RV had taken it or not. She was still an hour behind, and even if the RV had come down this way, they could be long gone by now.

Then, without warning, she rounded a curve and nearly collided with her RV's twin. The other vehicle let off a loud honk, and she swerved to the side to let it pass. The road was wide enough for two cars, but two large RVs was a narrow fit.

Her heart pounding and her palms prickling from the burst of adrenaline she had gotten, she let her RV sit along the shoulder for a moment, watching as the other one slowly disappeared in her side mirror. There was no question that it was the right one. She had found it—and it was getting away again.

Shaking herself out of her shock, she pulled back onto the road, already looking around for a place to turn around. There was nowhere obvious that she could do so without getting stuck, so she started driving again, and as she drove, she thought.

What had the other RV been doing back here? This was a secluded area without any shops or restau-rants. There were barely even any houses; the ones she saw were few and far between. There was no reason for the killer to come out here unless … unless it was to hide a body.

Tulia continued driving slowly, a sick certainty slowly growing inside her. She was too late; she had to be. The killer had been out here, alone, for an hour. What else would she have done, but claim another victim?

She hoped she was wrong, but she was certain she wasn't. Even if she could find a place to turn around —should she? If she followed the RV, what would happen to that poor man's body, if it really was out here?

But if she looked for his body instead of following the RV, would she be giving the killer time to find another victim?

This was too much for her to handle on her own. She needed police help, and she didn't know if anyone would take her seriously without proof. That man … there was no one to report him missing. No one to even notice he was missing, besides her. She needed to find him, both to give him justice and make sure he got a proper burial, and to give the police the evidence they needed to track this serial killer down.

Her mind made up, Tulia sped up a little, following the road. As she went farther and farther down it, it became more secluded. The man in the gas station said it led to state land, but she didn't know how far she would have to go to reach it. How far had the killer gone? Would she be able to tell where the other RV had stopped?

When she saw another vehicle pulled off onto the shoulder ahead of her, it took her a second to recognize it as not just any black SUV, but the one that had followed her through three states. Confused, she eased her RV to a stop behind it. What was Samuel doing here?

She looked around, but there were no houses in sight, nothing but trees and rocks and open spaces. Hesitantly, she got out of the RV. Other than the smell of the RV's exhaust, the air was fresh and clean. She wished she was getting ready to set up camp instead of looking for a dead body.

"Samuel?" she called out, still uncertain. It was the right SUV—she recognized the plate—but how had he found this place before she did?

Something moved in the trees to her left, and she jumped, turning to face the noise just as Samuel stepped out of the tree line. He had branches in his hair, and looked more tired than usual.

"Tulia?" His eyes went from her face to her RV and back again, full of suspicion.

"What are you doing here?" she asked.

"I could ask you the same question."

"I'm looking for that serial killer you told me about," she said, crossing her arms. "I think I saw her at a supermarket in Billings. She had a man with her, and I know she came this way."

"Describe the man you saw her with."

"He had a red baseball cap, short brown hair, blue eyes. He was wearing camo. He said he was trying to hitchhike to California. I think she's either going to kill him, or already did." Samuel hesitated, and her heart dropped. "Did … did you find him?"

She started forward toward where he had come out of the trees, and he moved to stop her. "Tulia, don't—"

She pushed past him, hurrying past the tree line. The bright red of his hat was the first thing she saw. Heartbroken, she stumbled forward, only stopping when she saw the gruesome wound on his neck. The killer had slashed his throat; she just hoped it had been quick. That was the only comfort she could wish on him now.

"Oh, no. Oh, my goodness."

She felt Samuel's strong arms on her shoulders as he pulled her back. Without thinking, she turned to him, and he pulled her into a hug.

"I was too late," she whispered. She'd known what to expect, but seeing it was different.

"So was I." He patted her back, and she made no move to pull away. She'd failed. They both had, but she'd had the killer in her sights.

And now, because she had been too slow, too hesitant, a man was dead. It was all her fault.

CHAPTER FIVE

Pulling herself together, Tulia took a deep breath and turned back toward the road, deliberately avoiding looking at the man's body. "I should call the police."

"I already called them," Samuel said. "I'm going to stay with the body until they arrive."

"Oh. Good." Suddenly, she turned and looked at him. "You don't still think *I* did this, do you?"

He raised an eyebrow. "If I did, we wouldn't be having this conversation. No, I got here just as the other RV was pulling away. It drove through a patch of soft, sandy soil along the shoulder, and I noted the tire tread marks. It has different tires than yours does. So, unless you managed to change all four tires in less than five minutes between when the killer left and you arrived, I believe you. Your … involvement in this is nothing but a coincidence."

"Well, I only got involved this time because you told me about this serial killer," she pointed out. "So, I wouldn't call that a coincidence. More like, it's your fault."

He gave a huff of quiet laughter. "Why did you follow her, anyway? Why not go to the police?"

"I tried. They didn't believe me." She rubbed a hand over her face. "When I started describing what I saw of the person and their RV, they thought I was describing myself. They asked if I was turning myself in, or if it was a prank. I knew the killer was getting farther and farther away, so I decided talking to them was a waste of time and took off. I wasn't fast enough, though. How did you find this place, anyway?"

He grinned. "You might have noticed you lost your tail. I spotted the other RV on the highway heading into North Dakota. I managed to slip one of those tracking medallions onto it, and I've been tailing it ever since. It relies on bouncing a signal off of a cell phone's Bluetooth function, and using the cell signal to send the location out. With cell service so spotty out here, I've had a hard time keeping track of her. I didn't even realize she picked anyone up.

The last notification I got about her location was a couple miles from here; by the time I narrowed down where she was, the killer was already leaving. I'll need to call Marc to get him up-to-date; I can't believe she was able to kill someone else."

"How's he doing, anyway?" Last she knew, the other private investigator had been shot and was in the hospital.

"Still recovering, but he's doing much better. I think he's done with this case, though; the agency I work for is thinking about sending someone else out to take his place, but I'm hoping this killer will be behind bars before too long."

"Yeah." Studiously not looking at the body, she nodded toward her vehicle. "I guess I'm going to … go? Unless you think I should stay and talk to the police. They might not believe your description of the killer and the getaway vehicle if I'm here, though—it *is* really farfetched that I just happen to match the exact description."

"Actually…" He hesitated. "Look, I don't want to put you in danger. But someone should follow her. If you can catch up, maybe keep her in your line of sight, but not get close enough for her to notice you, we could relate her location information to the police. Now, with the body and the two of us as eyewitnesses, we should have enough evidence that they can do something."

"What about that tracking medallion thing?" she asked.

"It's not reliable out here. The cell service is garbage."

"I don't want her to get away any more than you do," Tulia said, sighing. "I really hope she doesn't notice me following her, but I'll find her if I can."

"Don't put yourself in danger. As long as we know roughly where she is, the police will be able to find her."

"Okay," she said. "I'll do it. I'd better leave now. She's already gotten a head start."

"I think she'll keep heading west," he said as she started moving toward her RV. "Wait, let me give you my phone number. Call me if you spot her. And give me yours too; I'll call you once the police are done here."

She paused and exchanged numbers with him, then hurried back to her RV, worried that she was going to lose the killer's trail for good. She saw a clear, flat area a little way ahead where the other RV must have turned around, so she pulled ahead and painstakingly made the turn herself. Finally, she was pointed the right direction. Pausing for a second to wave goodbye to Samuel, who was still standing guard a respectful distance from the body, she hit the gas—just a little bit, since the RV didn't like bumpy dirt roads—and headed off after the killer.

At the end of the dirt road, she turned back toward the freeway, passing the small gas station and the tiny town of Columbus. She kept her eyes peeled as she drove, but it had been nearly half an hour, and the other RV was long since gone. She'd just have to hope that she and Samuel were right and that the RV was going west.

"I wish you could understand what we're doing," she said to Cicero as she drove. "I'm sorry you've been in your cage all day, buddy."

Everything was a mess. She was already miles from Billings, and could very well drive for miles more today, so she wouldn't get to explore it or any of the parks in the area. She'd wanted to hike the rimrocks and maybe even see a movie or something fun and just for her, but she doubted she would want to drive all the way back when she was done taking down the killer. She didn't even know where she would park for the night, but worrying about it made her feel selfish.

A man was dead, and in at least a small way, it was her fault.

It was a deceptively beautiful day. She could see why Montana was called Big Sky Country. The landscape opened up around her, endless and beautiful. In the research she'd done before visiting, she'd learned it was the sixth least populated state, and it showed. As the miles went past, she realized just how empty most of it was. No, not empty—there was plenty of nature, just not many cities. She wished she was making this drive in better circumstances; she would have enjoyed taking in the views so much more, with no lingering feeling of guilt and grief.

Despite the wide-open road, she saw no sign of the other RV. She knew there was no way she could catch up to it, but she'd still held out hope that the killer would have been delayed, somehow. She eyed the rest stops and the gas stations that hugged the freeway as she passed them, and while she saw a handful of RVs, none of them were the same distinctive model as hers.

When her fuel light came on, she bit back a sigh of frustration. She'd only put a little bit of gas in the RV before, since she'd wanted to hurry up and go after the killer. Now, she was going to pay for that by losing out on more time.

She took the next exit that had a sign for gas, and pulled into a station that was mostly populated by trucks. This time, she paid at the pump, and leaned against the side of the RV as the tank filled up. Checking her phone, she spotted a text message she hadn't seen while she was driving. It was from Samuel and had only been sent a few minutes before.

Got a ping from the tracker. Sending you a map pin. Looks like she's heading toward BLM land, maybe to camp. Let me know if you find her.

She checked her notifications, wondering how he was sending her the map location. She didn't see any new notifications—but then, she didn't currently have any bars of service. The map location must not have had a chance to come through before she lost the signal.

Feeling even more frustrated, she waited until the pump clunked off and replaced her fuel cap, then headed into the gas station.

"Excuse me," she said to the young woman at the counter. "Do you have maps? I'm trying to find some BLM land nearby, but I don't have any cell signal."

"Sure." The woman popped a bubble in the gum she was chewing, and pointed to a small shelf next to the counter. "Bring one over, and I can point out what you need. You camping?"

Tulia nodded, going to fetch a map. She had never actually camped on the land managed by the Bureau of Land Management, but she'd read that it was possible to camp for free on most of it, and she had seen some gorgeous photos of secluded spots.

"Right," the woman said, unfolding the map Tulia handed to her. "Well, we've got a couple million acres in Montana, but if you're looking for somewhere nearby to camp with that RV, there are probably only a few good spots. This one here is near a river." She took a red sharpie and drew a circle on the map. "And this here is right off the main road and has some good views. It's really flat; I see people camping with RVs there all the time."

"Thanks," Tulia said, peering at the map. "This is really helpful. And where are we now?"

The woman scrawled a sloppy star near one of the freeway exits, then handed the map over. "You got cash? Our card limit is ten bucks, so if not, you'll have to find some more stuff to buy."

All she had on her was the hundred. The thought of it made her jaw clench; it should have gone to helping that man on his trip across the country, but now he was dead. Filled with new resolve to track down the killer, she grabbed a few snacks and paid for her purchases, then strode back out to the RV.

With luck, the map pin Samuel had sent her would come through when she started driving and picked up a bar or two of service again. If it didn't, though, she would drive past every inch of BLM land in the area, and would keep going until she spotted the other RV.

She'd failed to save the man's life. She wasn't about to fail him a second time. The killer needed to be brought to justice.

CHAPTER SIX

She looked and looked, driving around to every patch of BLM land she could find. She kept checking her phone, but even when she had a couple bars of service, the map pin Samuel said he sent her never came through. She kept looking until the sun began to set, the wide-open sky painted in shades of pink and orange and purple. Finally, she had to give up. Samuel wasn't answering her texts or her calls, Cicero was bored out of his mind since he had been in his cage all day, and she needed to walk around, eat something, and take a few deep breaths. She didn't know if she had ever been this stressed out in her life.

Backtracking a bit, she returned to the stretch of BLM land the woman at the gas station had pointed out, which was within view of a small river. It was a gorgeous, secluded area, with enough flat space for her to park her RV and set up a folding table and a camp chair outside. Even though it was one of the most beautiful campsites she'd been to, she couldn't find it in her to relax.

"We'll find her tomorrow, won't we, buddy?" she asked her bird. Cicero let out a low whistle and fluttered his wings, staring eagerly at the open RV door. He was still in his cage, and while she planned on taking him out in his harness later, she wouldn't be able to eat with him on her shoulder. He was a relentless food thief and firmly believed that all food she had was his.

As a compromise, she carried his entire cage outside, setting it on top of the folding table and letting him enjoy the view while she went inside and microwaved her dinner. The RV had a small range and oven, but she didn't have the energy to actually cook something, so she was resorting to a frozen dinner tonight. She made herself some tea while she was at it, then took her drink and her dinner outside before popping back in to grab a cup full of Cicero's food. They ate their dinner together, Cicero safely in his cage, and slowly, Tulia felt the stress of the day begin to fade. It really was beautiful out here. It was strange to think that she'd been gone from home for a couple of months now. In some ways, she thought she was hardly recognizable as the person she used to be. In others, she didn't feel as if she had changed at all.

She certainly never would have thought she would spend a day chasing after a serial killer, and she wished she still hadn't had that experience. Maybe if she had actually managed to save that man, it would've been different, but right now, she just felt useless. She didn't even know his name. She knew nothing but a small sliver of his life's story.

She finished her food, packed up her trash, then took Cicero back inside so she could take him out of his cage and put his harness on him. He didn't fight her as much as he normally did—she often had to endure at least one bite as she pulled his wings through the specially made avian harness—and was already flapping his wings excitedly as she headed for the door, the loop of the elastic leash securely around her wrist.

Stepping outside, she took a deep breath, enjoying the fresh air and the scent of crushed vegetation from where she had driven her RV over the grass. Holding her hand up so Cicero could flap his wings and "fly" as they walked, she headed down toward the stream. At first, it seemed quiet out there, but as she got use to the lack of traffic, she realized it was actually quite noisy, with the hum of insects, the sounds of birds calling as they flew through the evening air, and the gurgle of the water as it passed over rocks. Somewhere in the distance, she heard a cow moo, and from far off, she heard a coyote yip.

It felt good to walk, and she meandered through the tall grass for a while, letting Cicero get some of his energy out. When he was done flapping, he settled down and simply looked around, seeming to observe the landscape with the same intensity she did. Once, she felt his claws grip her fingers tightly, and he turned his head, one pale silver-yellow eye looking up at the sky. She followed his gaze and saw, far above, some sort of big bird circle twice before it headed off away from them. The sky was a deep blue by now, and she knew it would be completely dark soon, so she headed back toward her RV.

She didn't know where the serial killer was, she didn't even know where Samuel was, but there was nothing she could do about it tonight. For now, it was just her, her bird, and miles of wilderness. This was what she had come on her trip for. Things might not have gone perfectly so far, but she was learning. Learning about her country and about herself.

She was tired, but she thought she would have time for a blog post tonight. She wouldn't talk about the serial killer, not until she knew more about what was going on. She didn't want to give the killer any clue that someone was on her tail, on the off chance that her blog reached the murderer's eyes. No, tonight she would post about the natural beauty of Montana and the way the wide-open sky made her feel small and infinite all at once.

Then, tomorrow, she'd be back at it. She was a waitress who'd gotten lucky with a lottery ticket—she definitely wasn't a professional when it came to solving crimes. But she cared about people, and she couldn't let a serial killer go without at least trying to bring them to justice.

Even though the area she was in was secluded, she made sure to lock her RV up tightly before she went to bed. While she knew it wasn't very likely that the serial killer would just happen to stumble upon her after she'd spent the day looking for her, she wasn't about to risk it.

No one disturbed her during the night, though, and when she woke up early in the morning, the area around her campsite was undisturbed. Dew clung to the tall grass, and she drank her coffee outside, enjoying the beginnings of another beautiful day. She checked her phone, but the tiny bar of service she'd had driving in had vanished, and while she could maybe find it again if she walked around for a while and waved her phone above her head, she decided to just pack up and head out. She was sure she would pick up service again on the main road, and hopefully Samuel would have some answers for her then, assuming he answered his phone.

She returned the folding table and chair to the RV, then looked around to make sure she hadn't left any trash or any of her other belongings behind, then took one last, long moment to look around and say a silent goodbye to her favorite camping spot yet before she carefully backed the RV up, turned around, and returned to the bumpy path that would take her to the road.

She was maybe a mile down the path when she spotted another vehicle coming toward her. It was only a few hundred feet away when she realized it was a police vehicle, and she pulled over as far as she could, intending to let them pass. She hoped she hadn't somehow camped in the wrong area, but she didn't think she had. She made sure she was in the same area the woman had circled, and she'd seen evidence that other people had camped there in the past. But the police vehicle didn't pass her—it's lights flicked on, and it pulled up in front of her. Two officers got out;

one approached and rapped on the driver's side window, and the other walked to the other side, out of sight. She rolled the window down, worried.

"I'm sorry if I camped in the wrong area," she began. "I thought this was BLM land and anyone could camp here for free."

"That's not why I'm pulling you over, miss," he said. "Do you have any firearms or other weapons on you?"

"I have a pocket knife in one of the drawers in the kitchen," she said. "And some pepper spray in my purse."

"I'm going to ask you to leave your purse in the vehicle and come out with your hands up," he said.

She felt sick with anxiety but did as he said. She knew she hadn't done anything wrong, especially not if she was camping in the right area, but she couldn't help but feel worried.

He carefully patted her down when she came out and then directed her to keep her hands on the hood of the RV. "We have a search warrant for this make of vehicle," he told her. "Before I go in, I'm going to ask you, is anyone else in there, or has anyone else been in there in the past week?"

"No, but I do have a pet bird. He's in his cage, but

he will probably bite if you put your fingers through the bars. Can I ask what this is about?"

"We will clarify matters in a moment, miss." He nodded at his partner and stepped into the RV to search it. She heard Cicero's insulted whistle then heard him say in Luis's voice, "What are you doing?" and felt bad for him. He'd never been particularly comfortable with strangers coming into his space.

The search didn't take very long; in just a few minutes, the officer returned, taking off a pair of gloves and shoving them in his pocket. He met his partner's eyes and shook his head. "Are you aware that someone called in a vehicle of this make and model with a driver matching your description in regards to a kidnapping and murder case?"

Suddenly, it all made sense. She straightened up and frowned. "Are you talking about a report made in Billings? Because I'm the one who made that report, and I practically got laughed out of the police station."

He raised an eyebrow. "That was one of the reports, yes. The other one was received yesterday evening. We'll have to clear that up with the other department. Do you have time to tell us the events surrounding the report you gave?"

She nodded, still irritated from the way she'd been

treated at the Billings police station but glad she was finally being taken seriously. She was guessing the person who had given the other report was Samuel, or the police officers who had been in charge of recovering the body. Taking a deep breath, she said, "It all started when I noticed some private investigators were following me back in Michigan…"

Maybe writing her blog had made her into a wordier person than she used to be, but it took her a long time to tell the story, and she was complete enough that the officers barely had any questions when she was done. It felt good to finally be able to tell the whole story. She had been worried at first that the officers wouldn't believe her, but it turned out that Samuel had mentioned her in his report, and the Billings police department verified their portion of her story. Having found no evidence that anyone other than her had even been in it, they were willing to let her go.

"Thank you for cooperating, miss," the officer said, finally shaking her hand and handing her his card. "If you do happen to see that other RV again, please give us a call. We will enter your license plate number into our report, and you shouldn't be bothered again, but if you are, feel free to have the officers give me a call. I hope you enjoy the rest of your trip."

She thanked him, pocketed the card, then watched as they turned their vehicle around and headed away. How they'd found her, she didn't know, but she supposed her RV was rather notable. Anyone could've seen her turn off the main road, or, for all she knew, they'd been driving around looking for her for hours.

As she climbed back behind the driver's wheel, it was with a certain sense of satisfaction. The police were finally looking for the serial killer. They might not have been fast enough to save that poor man from being murdered, but at least with his body and her and Samuel's eyewitness accounts, the authorities had enough evidence to start doing something about it. She and Samuel weren't the only ones looking for the serial killer anymore.

CHAPTER SEVEN

She drove until she hit the next town, where she had two bars of service, and decided to indulge herself in a gooey cinnamon roll from a tiny café while she called Samuel. She didn't have any missed calls or text messages from him, which was concerning, but she figured he probably just hadn't been in an area with cell service. With any luck, this call would go through. She wanted to tell him about her interaction with the police, and let him know they were finally on the lookout for the serial killer he had been hunting. She was sure he would want to tell Marc. Even though his partner was sitting this one out, he would want to be kept up to date.

After her cinnamon roll was delivered to her table,

she dialed Samuel's number and waited for the call to ring through.

Instead of ringing, however, it went straight to voicemail. Frowning, she tried again. The same thing happened. Did that mean that he was still in a no-service area? Sighing, she gave up and sent him a text message instead, telling him the police had talked to her and were looking for the other RV.

She was worried about him, but even if something had happened to him, there was no way for her to know. She would just have to wait for him to contact her again.

She tried to push the thoughts out of her mind as she enjoyed the food. After finishing her meal, she left the hundred-dollar bill she had gotten for the man whose murder she had tried to prevent as a tip and left, settling back into the RV with Cicero.

"Well, buddy, I guess we're on our own again," she said, sitting on the couch. She had her phone in her hand and was already scrolling through the search results for local attractions. "We've lost both the serial killer and Samuel, and until one of them pops up on our radar, we might as well enjoy our trip."

As she scrolled, one of the links caught her eye. It was for a local rodeo. Her conversation with the woman at the supermarket came back to her. She frowned for a moment, remembering that the woman, Olivia, had similar hair and eye color to her—in other words, she matched the description of the serial killer. But she had been so nice, and Tulia didn't know why someone her age would have suddenly started committing murders left and right. She doubted most serial killers made it to their fifties before committing a crime, but all of the murders linked to the killer she was chasing seemed to have happened in the last year or two.

Even if she was a serial killer, it wouldn't help Tulia now, and it didn't mean the woman's advice hadn't been good. She was here, out west. The rodeo season wouldn't last forever. She might as well see one while she could.

She followed the link to the website and scrolled down to the FAQ. Under the Pets section, it said they were only allowed in certain areas, which she supposed made sense. They wouldn't want to worry about someone's dog getting off the leash and attacking a prize horse or bull.

She bit her lip, considering. She could go to the rodeo with Cicero—it was only an hour or so farther west from where she was now—and walk around with him in the areas he was allowed. Then, she could put him back in the RV with the air-conditioning running to keep him nice and cool, and watch some of the other attractions. She wasn't sure how she felt about stuff like bull riding, since it didn't seem very fun for the animal, but she was sure there were plenty of other things to see. It would be a once-in-a-lifetime experience for her— and this whole trip was about once-in-a-lifetime experiences.

Her mind made up, she copied the address and typed it into her GPS, then buckled herself into the driver's seat. Maybe, if the rodeo was anything like the fairs were back home, she could get an elephant ear while she was there.

The parking lot at the rodeo was busy, but to her pleasant surprise they had RV spots with electric hookups around the edges. She suspected they were meant for people traveling out of state to compete, but for a ten-dollar fee, she was able to park and plug her vehicle in. It gave her peace of mind. This way, she wouldn't have to worry about the generator's fuel level to keep Cicero nice and cool while she enjoyed the rodeo. First, though, he would have a chance to take in some of the sights on the outskirts.

She got his harness on and paid her entry fee, smiling at everyone's compliments towards the bird. He was always a hit when they went out, and while he didn't enjoy people getting too close to him, he did seem to enjoy their attention from a distance.

She walked around with him for a while, looking at the games and rides, and some of the more casual animal competitions. There was a dock-diving setup for dogs, where people could let their dogs jump into a pool after toys, with the winner being the one who jumped the farthest. She watched that for a while, letting Cicero sit on her shoulder while she applauded each and every dog, whether they bellyflopped into the pool or jumped farther than she thought possible. Both the people and the pets seemed to be having fun, but there wasn't anything here for Cicero to do, so after a bit, she continued walking on. When she noticed Cicero seemed to be getting a little over-whelmed with all the noise and chaos, she made her way back to the RV, drawing the blinds, putting up the sunshade, and chopping up a few grapes and slicing part of a banana for him before settling him in his cage. It was good for him to see the world and have new experiences, but he wasn't as comfortable with new situations as something like a dog would be. Some time to relax while she explored would do him good.

"I'll be back later, buddy," she said. "You take a nap, all right?"

"Good boy, good night," he said, a phrase he'd learned years ago. She smiled, repeated it back to him, and left, making sure to lock the RV behind her. Now, it was time to see what she really wanted to see: the horses.

She made her way back through the rodeo, finding an information stand with a schedule of events. The barrel racing was about to end, but the same arena was holding a mounted target shooting competition in a little while, which sounded neat.

She had to ask for directions twice, but finally she found the correct arena. It was the tail end of the barrel racing contest, and she found a seat in the middle of the bleachers to watch. Three people were riding into the ring: a man on a red-colored horse, a woman with blonde hair on a speckled white one—she wasn't a horse expert but she thought the color was Appaloosa—and another woman with darker hair on a pale blonde horse. Palomino? She'd have to look up horse colors later.

"Coming in third place with a time of nineteen point three seconds is Hannah Goddard and her horse, Sprite."

The woman with dark hair on the Palomino horse trotted forward and accepted a medal from the announcer, then cantered around the ring once before exiting. The man called out again, this time calling up the man on his red horse. Finally, he announced the winner, "And in first place, with an impressive time of fourteen point three seconds, is Ava Adkins and her horse, Tracker. Congratulations Ava, we hope to see you again next year."

Ava trotted up to accept the medal and cantered around the ring once. Tulia's eyes followed her, the name too familiar. Adkins... Wasn't that the last name of Olivia, the woman she had talked to at the supermarket? The woman had said her daughter was a rodeo star. She narrowed her eyes. It was hard to see from this distance, but she could tell that Ava had hair that was the same blonde as hers, and her eyes looked too dark to be blue. In other words, she must look very similar to Tulia. And while Tulia hadn't spotted her RV's twin in the parking lot, the rodeo's parking area was huge, and she hadn't exactly been looking. She knew enough about horses to know they were expensive—which meant that it wasn't impossible that a rodeo star would be able to afford the same type of RV she had. Was the RV hers? Was the woman who was currently riding her horse around the ring in front of a huge audience a murderer?

Ava finally rode out of the ring, and a handful of people started clearing the barrels out of the way to make room for the next event. Instead of staying to watch, Tulia got up and climbed down from the stands, hoping to find Ava in the crowd. She wasn't sure where the horse people went after competing, and it took her a while to finally find the barn. She half expected someone to stop her when she went inside, but no one did; people were too busy tending to their own horses and getting ready for events to pay any attention to her. She kept her eyes peeled for blonde hair and saw several people with the correct hair color, but none of them were Ava. She finally located the spotted horse, Tracker, with a handwritten name placard on his stall, but the woman was nowhere in sight. Tulia lingered as long as she could until a man approached. He had greying blond hair that was pulled back in a short ponytail and a weather-lined face. He patted Tracker's nose, then turned to her.

"Can I help you, ma'am?"

"I wanted an autograph," Tulia said, using the lie she'd settled on to explain her presence here if anyone asked. "From the woman who was riding him." She nodded at the horse.

"No autographs. Fans aren't supposed to be back here. I'm going to have to ask you to leave."

She muttered a quick apology before ducking out

of the stable, not wanting to draw attention to herself. Maybe it was just a coincidence, but the more she thought about it, the more it made sense. Ava traveled around the country competing with her horse. If she really was a famous figure in the industry, she must make good money. She matched Tulia's description, she might be able to afford the same RV, and she seemed to be traveling west at about the same rate Tulia had been.

Some things still didn't make sense, though. Who transported the horse, if Ava drove in the RV? Tulia felt like she was onto something. If she couldn't find Ava, maybe she could find the RV. The rodeo was still going strong, but none of the attractions appealed to her anymore since she didn't know how close she might be to finding the killer once and for all.

CHAPTER EIGHT

Even after walking through the entire parking lot
twice, she didn't see a match for her RV. It was frus-
trating; she didn't know if that meant the other
woman had left—without her horse; maybe she had
hired someone to drive it for her—or if it meant she
wasn't the killer. Finally giving up, she returned to
her own RV and took advantage of her air conditioning while she tried to figure out what to do next.
She thought that, with confirmation that the police
were on the case, she would be able to let it go, but it
seemed that she couldn't. She hated not being able to
do anything. For all she knew, the killer was out there
somewhere selecting her next victim. The worst part
was, it might be someone no one would even notice
was missing. Since this killer targeted the transient

population, there was no telling how many victims they had. Tulia hated the thought that some victims might not be found for years, if ever. It was another good reason to want the killer behind bars; maybe she would be able to give the authorities a true account of her victims and make sure they were all laid to rest properly.

Sighing, she picked up her phone to look for a place to camp that evening. She needed to refill the RV's water tanks and flush the sewage system, so she wanted an actual campground, somewhere with RV hookups. There were plenty to choose from, especially since she didn't mind driving a couple of hours for the right one. One of the campgrounds offered a pool, and she was clicking through the website and looking at pictures to see if it was something she wanted to drive out to when her phone screen changed to signify an incoming call. Samuel's name on the screen made her heart leap, and she pressed the button to answer it.

"Thank goodness, I have a lot to tell you," she said.

She waited for Samuel to respond, but instead only heard a strange thudding sound on the other end, and the growl of an engine. She hesitated. "Samuel?"

She heard someone exclaim—it was a sharp

voice, and sounded like a woman—then the line went dead. Confused, she tried calling him back, but the call only rang a couple of times before getting sent to voicemail.

"What on earth?" she muttered. She sent him a text message and waited, but there was no reply. She hadn't been truly worried about him before; he had told her his cell service was spotty out here. She thought he was just in an area without good service, maybe camping or regrouping at a motel. But now, she was beginning to wonder if something was seriously wrong.

She had no way of finding out more, though. She thought about calling Marc, but she didn't have his number, and besides, he was still healing from being shot. He might be able to give her the contact information for the agency they worked for, but she doubted they would know much more about Sam's current whereabouts than she did.

Feeling helpless for probably the hundredth time that week, she backed out of the website she had been on for the campground with the pool and instead found a closer local one. Regardless of everything else that was going on, she needed somewhere to sleep, but this way she would be closer to Samuel's last known location just in case he called her back and needed help. Not having anything else to do at the rodeo—knowing the killer may have slipped through her fingers again kind of dampened the experience for her—she headed out, driving in silence since she wasn't in the mood to listen to music or do anything but brood.

The campground she arrived at was boring but functional, with rows of RVs and campers in a field. There were no great views or beautiful paths to follow, but it would give her a place to sleep for the night and to refill her water tanks, so she wasn't complaining too much. After setting up, she opened the RVs windows to let a breeze in through the screens, then sat on the couch with her laptop on her lap. She tried calling Samuel again, but the call went straight to voicemail, and she decided to try to put it out of her mind for now as she worked on her latest blog post. Once again, she avoided mentioning anything about the serial killer. Instead, she detailed the rodeo and added some pictures she had taken, including one with her and Cicero. She made sure her face wasn't fully in the photo – she was still a little bit leery about sharing her full identity online for anyone to see—and wished she had gotten the chance to see more events. The horseback target shooting event sounded like it would have been fun.

After posting, she started going through some of her old posts, replying to comments. She had blocked anonymous comments, so only people with an account could leave comments. It meant fewer people interacted with her posts, but unfortunately, ever since her ex-boyfriend, Luis, had tracked her down, it had been a necessity. He had cheated on her, broken her heart, and still, for some reason, thought he was entitled to some of her lottery winnings. She wished she had the energy to laugh in his face and tell him how ridiculous he was, but when it came down to it, she just didn't want to deal with him.

Every time she checked her blog, she had more followers. She was getting close to ten thousand, which seemed wildly impressive to her. Her newest post had several new comments on it. Most of them were just people admiring the views of the camp site she'd stayed at the night before, but one caught her eye.

It's important. Call me. – M

Below it was an unfamiliar number. The comment had been posted just an hour ago. She stared at it for a moment, trying to figure out who it could be, before it clicked. M. That must stand for Marc. He must be worried about Samuel too. To verify her guess, she looked up the area code and confirmed it came from a state on the East Coast, where Samuel and Marc had started their investigation from. It had to be Marc's cell phone number.

Hoping she was right and she wasn't about to call some complete stranger, she typed the number on her phone and hit the call button. It only rang once before someone answered. She hadn't spoken to Marc as much as she had spoken to Samuel—he seemed to be quieter and less interested in engaging with the people around him—but she recognized his voice when he spoke.

"Hello?" He sounded worried.

"Hi. Marc, right? It's me. Tulia."

He let out a sigh of relief. "Thank goodness. I was beginning to worry you wouldn't see the comment. Do you know you have someone looking for you?"

She blinked. "I do?"

"A man called me about ten minutes ago. He must have gotten my number from the comment I left on your post. He said his name was John and he wanted to know if I knew where you were."

"I don't think I know any Johns," she said. Well, she had an uncle named John, but he had her number, and she only ever saw him on holidays, so she doubted he'd try to reach her in such a roundabout way.

"I looked up the number after I got off the phone with him, and it belongs to a small private investigative firm in Michigan. Don't worry, I didn't tell him anything, but I thought you should know."

"Luis must've hired him," she said. Anger bubbled inside her. She wished he would just leave her alone. He'd made his decision. If he'd done the bare minimum of being a good boyfriend—such as not cheating on her, he would've been sharing in her wealth right now. She didn't feel anything for him except anger and hurt. "My ex," she added belatedly when she realized Marc probably didn't know who that was. Or maybe he did; he and Samuel had, at one point, been investigating her under suspicion of kidnapping and murder and had probably done some digging once they learned her name.

"I'd watch out for him, then. I don't know why he's after you, but if it's to the point where he's hiring private investigators, it can't be good. Anyway, that's not why I called. Have you seen Samuel? I know he had a run-in with you, but I haven't heard from him since."

"He told you about the body we found, right?"

"Yes. He reported back to me after the police left the scene. That's the last I heard from him."

"That's the last I heard from him too." Her

stomach twisted with worry. "No, wait. It's not. He texted me a couple hours after that, saying he'd gotten a ping from the tracker he put on the killer's RV. He said he was sending me the map pin, but it never came through. I also got a weird call from him about an hour ago, but he didn't say anything. The call just ended after a few seconds."

"I think he's in trouble. I hate to ask you this, but could you drive by a location for me and tell me what you see? I'm not sure how close you are to it. I'm guessing you're still in Montana, at least. I can send you the money for gas, or whatever you need. I think he could be in real danger."

"Don't worry about money. I can go drive by it, even if it's not close to me." It wasn't as if she was following a strict schedule. She was worried about Samuel too, and if she could help, she wanted to.

"This is your cell phone number, correct?" he asked.

"Yes."

"I'm going to hang up, and I'll send you a location. It's a location that Samuel shared with me a couple hours ago, without explanation. I tried calling him after he sent it but got no response, and he hasn't been answering my texts. I don't know if he sent it by accident, or if something else is going on, but if he's in trouble, it could be his way of asking for help."

"Okay. I'll text you once I get it. I'll let you know how far away I am, too."

"Thanks, Tulia," Marc said. "And good luck."

He ended the call. She checked that the bars of service she had were strong, then set her phone down on the arm of the couch and stared at it, waiting for the message from Marc to come through.

CHAPTER NINE

The location Marc sent her was about an hour north of where she was. There were GPS coordinates that led to a random road in the middle of nowhere; something she didn't think was a great sign. Hoping all of this was a misunderstanding, and Samuel was just in an area with little to no phone service, she detached her RV from the hookups and started it up, pulling out of the campground and heading back onto the main road. It was dark out, and Cicero was drowsy, so she played soft music as she drove, hoping the bird wouldn't pick up on her anxiety.

Even though she'd driven more in the past few months than she ever had before, something about the hour drive north felt longer than any other drive she had made. When her GPS alerted her that she was coming up to a turn, she took it, then glanced at the phone screen. She was only a couple of miles away from where Samuel's last known location was. Her gut twisted with nerves. She had no idea what to expect. The fact that she hadn't heard from him for so long was beginning to feel more ominous. She wished she had done something about it sooner, though she didn't know what that something should have been. She hadn't had Marc's number, and she didn't actually know what agency they worked for, or if he had a family she should call.

Her nerves only got worse as she drew closer. Soon, she was two turns away, then one. Then, finally, she turned onto the road the coordinates Marc had sent her were on. It wasn't a dirt road, but it wasn't a busy road either. With two narrow lanes of cracked asphalt and few houses around, but plenty of cattle and horses, it was beyond secluded. By now, the sky was pitch black except for the stars, and the sense of solitude was crushing.

She eased off the gas as the map marker got closer and closer on her GPS. Letting the RV coast, she finally pulled to a stop along the shoulder just past where the marker was. She hadn't seen anything— there were no stranded vehicles, and thankfully, no obvious signs of a body. Her whole body seemed to tingle with unease as she turned on her hazards and, slowly, climbed out of the RV and onto the shoulder of the road. Shadows seemed to loom all around her as she walked back toward the GPS marker, and she tried very hard not to think of the various horror movies and murder documentaries she had seen throughout her life.

She scoured the ground, looking in the long grass for … she didn't know what. A footprint, a drop of blood, *something.* She almost missed the black rectangle of an abandoned phone when her own phone's flashlight revealed it the first time, and swung the light back around to pinpoint it.

Kneeling down, she picked it up and turned it over in her hands. She didn't know Samuel well enough to recognize his phone by sight, but she was willing to bet it was his. The screen was cracked, and it didn't turn on when she pressed the buttons, but she held out hope that was just because it had run out of battery.

Going back to her RV, she settled into the driver's seat and plugged the phone into her own phone charger. The screen glowed after a second, showing a lightning bolt, and she felt a rush of relief. It was charging. Maybe they'd have some answers soon.

While she waited for the phone to charge enough

to turn on, she called the number Marc had called her from. He answered almost immediately. "Did you find him?"

"I found his phone," she said, looking down at it. "At least, I'm pretty sure it's his phone. The screen is cracked, but it still works, and it's charging."

"Shoot. Can you get into it? Maybe there's some information on it we can use to find him."

"Just a second."

She tried holding down the power button, and this time, it turned on. The lock screen photo was of a small stream, too generic for her to be able to tell who the phone belonged to. Hopeful that maybe he hadn't set it up to lock with a passcode, she dragged the screen up, but it asked her for a pin.

"The screen's locked. Do you know what his passcode is?"

"No idea," Marc said. "Hold on, let me call it. That way we can be sure it's his phone, at least."

He said a quick goodbye and hung up. A moment later, his number came up on the phone in front of her. She hit the button to answer it, confirmed the phone was Samuel's, then hung up. He called her back on her own phone.

"So, you found Samuel's phone, but no sign of

him. There wasn't any blood or signs of a struggle nearby?"

"No. I looked, but I didn't see anything," she said. "It was just off the shoulder of the road, like someone had thrown it out a car window."

"Shoot." He bit back a sound that sounded like a groan. "Sorry, being shot really sucks, I don't recommend it. I wish I was there, though my wife would kill me if she heard me saying that. I feel so useless not being able to do anything. Something's wrong. He wouldn't go this long without contacting the agency."

"What should I do?" she asked, twisting in her seat and staring out through the windshield. Montana had never felt so big. "Try to call the police and tell them he's missing?"

"That should probably be the next step, but I don't know if they'll be much help. They won't be able to track him with his phone, obviously, and I'm guessing you're not in an area that's likely to have security cameras or traffic cameras they could use to look for him."

She looked around. There was no sign of any human habitation except for some fence posts and, a little bit further down, a billboard. It was old and faded, as if it hadn't been changed for years.

"Yeah, I don't think we're going to find any cameras out this way."

Something about the billboard caught her eye. The woman on it was familiar—she could've sworn it was Ava Adkins, the woman she'd seen at the rodeo earlier. Even though the billboard itself was faded, she could still make out the woman's features. Beneath it, in cracked and peeling letters were the words, *Adkins Ranch, 5 miles ahead! Visit for trail rides, leave with memories that last a lifetime.*

"Hold on," she murmured. "I think… I think I know where the serial killer lives."

"What? How did you figure that out?"

"There's a billboard—" she broke off, shaking her head. It would take too long to tell him the entire story. "Look, just do a search for Ava Adkins. She does a rodeo show—barrel racing and maybe some other stuff, I don't know. I think she's pretty big in the rodeo circuit, and she might have done something on the East Coast for a while. Something involving horses, I think."

"You think this Ava lady is the killer?" he sounded skeptical. "She sounds a bit more high profile than we'd normally expect for a serial killer."

"I know it doesn't make much sense, but it all lines up. I ran into her mother at the supermarket a while back, and I saw Ava earlier today, and—look, I'll tell you about it later. Just … look her up. See if she was on the East Coast when those murders happened. I have to get going. I think I know where to find Samuel, if the killer took him."

"Hey, hold on. You shouldn't be doing this yourself. I'm as worried about Samuel as you are—probably more so; I've worked with the man for five years now. But I know he wouldn't want you to get hurt trying to save him."

"He doesn't get a say," Tulia snapped. "I already let one man die because I was too slow. I'm not letting it happen a second time. Remember. Ava Adkins."

With that, before he could protest more, she hung up the phone. Staring at the billboard, she pulled away from the shoulder and turned off her blinkers as she got up to speed.

If Samuel was nearby, she was going to find him. She wouldn't be too late this time.

CHAPTER TEN

She followed the directions on the sign, squinting to see the road signs in the dark. It felt like a longer drive than it should have been, and with darkness encroaching from all sides, the only light the stark flood of the RV's bright headlights on the road in front of her, she began to wish she was anywhere but here. When she was listening to music on the road in the middle of the day, it was easy to forget just how sparsely populated this area of the country was. Now, though, she was keenly aware of just how alone she was out here.

Finally, she saw the wooden sign declaring the entrance to Adkins Ranch. As she slowed the RV, Cicero woke up from his nap, fluttering his wings once and letting out a whistle that made her wince.

"Sorry, bud," she said as she turned onto the driveway. "You should go back to sleep." African grey parrots were diurnal birds, and usually went to bed with the sun. She felt bad for keeping him up so long, but there wasn't another option. Samuel was in danger, and she couldn't wait until morning to save him. She might already be too late.

The driveway was a long, dirt one, with wooden livestock fences to either side of it, making her feel penned in. As she started down the long drive, she felt the prickle of unease. She'd come out here with no real plan besides tracking down Samuel, and was well aware that she might be driving directly into the serial killer's lair. Letting the RV slow to a crawl and then a stop, she paused to check her phone, wondering if she should call the police. Her phone decided for her; she had no service here.

She considered backing up and finding somewhere she did have service, but there was nowhere to turn around, and with her car being towed behind her, she didn't think she would be able to make it out of the driveway without hitting something, probably the fence. And if there really was a serial killer out here, the last thing she wanted to do was make them angry by destroying their property.

The only way to go was forward. Cautiously, she

let up on the brake and let the RV begin to move again. Before long, the driveway curved, and then she saw lights ahead of her. There were two structures; a large barn with a floodlight high up on its side, and a single-story ranch house. There were friendly, warm lights in the windows and a couple of vehicles parked out front. She looked for the RV, and at first, she didn't see it. Maybe this was the wrong place after all; she could just turn around in the open area up ahead and leave, or apologize to the homeowners if they came out to see who she was.

But then, she spotted a shadowy shape under the barn's floodlight. It was a covered vehicle, so she couldn't see the color of the paint or the shape of the body, but it looked like the exact dimensions of her own RV—something she had gotten to know very well over the past couple of months—and she would be willing to bet just about anything that it was the RV she had been hunting for all week.

This was it. This was the place. This was where Samuel and Marc's serial killer came home to roost. And, unfortunately for her, this was where she was most likely to find Samuel—if he was even still alive.

Only the knowledge that if she waited any longer she might be too late—that she might *already* be too late—kept her going down the driveway. Well aware that whoever was inside the house would notice the RV soon if they hadn't already, she pulled into the open area in front of the house and turned around in a big circle, leaving the RV pointing out in the very likely chance that she needed to make a quick exit. Then, she grabbed her pepper spray, her phone, and her keys, and said one last goodbye to Cicero.

"I'll be back, buddy," she promised quietly as she slipped out the RV's door, pausing to lock it behind her.

She turned, intending to go up to the house and do —well, she didn't know what—and let out a strangled scream when she realized a man was standing right behind her. It wasn't Samuel—of course, it wouldn't be that easy. He was a middle-aged man, with a weather-lined face and graying blond hair drawn back into a short ponytail. He was the same man who had confronted her earlier, at the fair, though he didn't seem to recognize her. She eyed the hair for a second, wondering. She, Samuel, and Marc all talked about the serial killer as if they were a woman, since the description in the news articles was always of a woman with long blonde hair, but was it possible people had been seeing this man instead?

Then, he spoke, and she had to scramble to come up with a plausible reason for her presence. "Can I help you, ma'am?" he asked, his tone more curious than wary. He eyed her RV, and she thought she caught his eyes dart over toward the covered vehicle near the barn, but the movement was too fast for her to be certain.

"I—I'm lost," she managed. "I saw the billboard, and I thought this was a public business. I'm sorry, I didn't realize it was someone's home. I thought I might find someone I could ask for directions."

"That old thing," he said, shaking his head. "I keep telling them they should take it down. We don't offer tours anymore, or trail rides. But I think we can offer some directions. Where is it that you're looking to get to?"

That was a great question. Tulia said the first thing that came to mind. "I'm looking for BLM land to camp on. I'm taking a trip across the country, you see, and I thought I could make a few more hours tonight, but I didn't realize how hard it would be to find a camping spot once it was dark."

"You're in the middle of a lot of private land out here," he said, sucking on his cheeks before continuing. "I think the best thing for you to do will be to pull out of the drive and turn left, heading down the road a couple of miles until you reach—"

He broke off at the creaking sound of the screen

door opening, and they both turned to look at the house. Up on the porch, looking out of the front door, was a young woman about Tulia's age. Ava, Tulia thought, though she looked different than the woman on the billboard. "Who is it, Levi?" she called out.

"Just a woman asking for directions," he called back. "I'm helping her out, then I'm going to head home."

"Is that her RV? Hold on, tell her to wait. Mom's got to see this."

The screen door slammed shut, and Tulia heard the woman calling for her mom. If this really was Ava, who she'd only ever seen at a distance or on TV, her mother must be Olivia. She felt her heart rate kick up a notch. Would the other woman recognize her? She really should have thought this through better. But still, the worry about Samuel urged her forward. This might be dangerous, but if he really had been taken by the killer, it was nothing compared to the danger he was in. At least she hadn't been selected as a victim—yet.

"You might as well come on up to the porch," Levi said with a sigh. "They're going to want to talk, I'm sure. What's your name?"

"Tulia," she said, giving him a quick handshake as they walked. "Tulia Blake." Maybe she should have come up with a fake name, but she had already stumbled through a few bad lies and didn't want to come off as any more suspicious than she knew she already was.

"Well, Ms. Blake, I'm Levi Seaver, head ranch hand around here and family friend of the Adkins women. You a fan of rodeo?"

"I went to my first one not long ago," she said. "I'd like to see more, I didn't get to stay long."

"Well, at least you're not one of their crazy fans," he said with a chuckle. "They get some strange people out here. Come on up onto the porch, watch your step there, that board's loose. You can take a seat on the swing if you want, I don't know how long they'll be."

Tulia sat on the porch swing, looking out into the darkness. In the barn, a horse whinnied. It was peaceful out here; peaceful and quiet. She could imagine coming out here on a misty morning to drink her coffee, surrounded by acres and acres of land.

In any other circumstance, she would have loved being here. A real ranch! But now, she could only wonder if she was going to get out of here alive … and if Samuel was somewhere on the property, waiting for her to find him.

CHAPTER ELEVEN

It didn't take long before she heard footsteps inside, and the woman she was almost certain was Ava opened the screen door. She spotted Tulia, smiled, then gestured at the RV, stepping back so the woman behind her could come out as well.

"Mom, look, she has the same RV as—"

But the woman—yes, she was Olivia—wasn't looking at the RV. She glanced at Tulia and then did a double take. Her eyes narrowed.

"I saw you at the grocery store the other day, didn't I?"

"She didn't say she's from the area. I thought you said you were traveling?" Levi said, frowning. "You don't sound like a local."

"I'm not, I—" Tulia began, but Olivia continued.

"It was the day we stopped for lunch, Ava. At the supermarket in Billings."

Ava's eyes widened. "Are you sure?"

They were all looking at Tulia now, and she felt herself begin to flush. "I mean, maybe? I did stop there, I had to get some groceries, but I don't remember talking to anyone there." Her words rang false to her own ears, but she hoped that was just because she knew she was lying. With any luck, the others would believe her.

"I don't like this," Olivia said. Finally, she looked toward the RV, and the concern on her face only deepened. "That RV. Where did you get it?"

"I bought it," Tulia said. "About three months ago. Look, I really didn't mean to make any trouble. I was just looking for directions."

"I don't believe you," Olivia said. She crossed her arms. "What are you really doing here? Are you a stalker? Are you stalking my daughter? She's had enough of that."

"No," Tulia said, standing up. "I swear, I'm not. I'm just—look, I'm looking for someone. A guy. His name is Samuel, and he went missing. A friend of his got a notification that his phone was near here, and I drove up to see if I could figure out what was going on. I found the phone on the side of the road."

"Well, we didn't have anything to do with that," Ava said, crossing her arms. "If your friend is missing, maybe you should call the police, not skulk around here."

"I don't think she's the one who should be calling the police," Olivia said, her lips pressed together. "She's trespassing on our property. I'm going to go and get my phone, and you better be gone by the time I'm back."

Olivia went back inside, the screen door slamming behind her. Levi shifted uncomfortably, rubbing his hand over the back of his neck. "Sorry, miss, looks like you better get going. I'll see you off the property."

"I keep telling Mom we should take down that billboard," Ava said, sighing. "I can't count the number of times it's brought strangers here, thinking the ranch was still open to the public." She met Tulia's eyes. "Look, I don't know if you're telling the truth or not. If your friend really is missing, I'm sorry, but he isn't here. And if you're another stalker, here because you saw me or my mom at a rodeo, just leave, please? We've had enough of all that. We don't do tours or trail rides anymore, we aren't selling horses, and we aren't giving any lessons. And no, you can't have an autograph. I just got home after doing a tour across the country, and I want to decompress."

"My friend really is missing," Tulia said. She met Ava's gaze, trying to imagine this woman as a serial killer. She couldn't, but Luis had proven to her that she wasn't the best judge of people. "You said you were touring around the country? Did you spend much time out East?"

"Yeah," Ava said, raising an eyebrow. "I started the tour in Georgia, went up the East Coast, and then came back out West. It wasn't all rodeo, of course; most of it was putting on shows and doing seminars to help people with their horses."

"What vehicle did you drive during your tour?" Tulia asked, darting a glance at the covered RV next to the barn.

"I don't see how that's relevant," Ava said, crossing her arms. Behind her, in the barn, a horse whinnied again and a moment later, several other horses joined in. Sighing, she turned to Levi. "Will you please go check that out? They've been acting up all evening, ever since Mom put Tracker in his stall."

"Sure thing," Levi said, shooting a cautious glance at Tulia. "You want me to see her off the property first?"

Tulia could feel her pulse in the skin of her

fingers. This wasn't going according to plan. She had gotten too sidetracked, too distracted by their accusations. She needed to find Samuel, and she was certain he was here.

"You said the horses have been acting up all evening?" Tulia asked. "Is there someone in there?"

"Why would there be anyone in the barn?" Ava asked.

"Like I said, I'm looking for my friend. I have reason to believe he's here."

"And you think he might be hiding in our barn." Ava threw up her hands. "Fine, come see the horses with us. But then please just leave. My mom is serious, she's going to call the cops if you're still here when she comes out. This is our private property, and we have a right to privacy."

Gritting her teeth against a feeling of embarrassment and chagrin, she followed Levi and Ava across the yard toward the barn. Inside, the horse whinnied, and they heard a thunk, as if it had kicked the stall door. "They really are upset," Ava murmured. She sent a glance back at Tulia and frowned. "Open it up, Levi. Let's see what has them so unsettled."

CHAPTER TWELVE

Levi pulled, the big wooden door rattling as it opened. Reaching inside, he tugged at a cord and an overhead light came on. He stepped inside, Ava and Tulia following him. Ava seemed jumpy, and Tulia kept her eyes on her; surely, both of them couldn't be involved in the murders, right? But what if she was wrong about that? What if everyone here was involved, and she was being led into a trap? Her hand tightened on her pepper spray. It felt like a very inadequate weapon.

The interior of the barn was hardpacked dirt sprinkled with dry straw. She saw the curious heads of a couple of horses looking out over their stalls, and one of them whinnied in greeting. Levi walked over to the horse and patted it on the cheek, looking around. "I don't see anything," he said. "Might've been a raccoon or something, I guess."

"Maybe we should set one of those live trips," Ava suggested, peering around. "If it is a raccoon, we don't want it getting too comfortable."

"I'll come out tomorrow and do it," Levi said. "I've really got to get going, my wife expected me—"

He broke off and turned to stare at the sound of something thudding against the door of an apparently empty stall. Ava took half a step back, her eyes widening. "There's something in there," she hissed. Levi took a hesitant step forward, a frown creasing his brow, but Tulia pushed past him, suddenly certain of what, or who, she was going to find. Running forward, she nearly slammed into the stall door in her hurry to look over it.

"Samuel," she breathed, staring at the man inside. He was bound at his wrists and ankles and gagged, lying on his side in the straw. He kicked the stall door again, and looked at her, his eyes wild.

"What the…" Levi joined her, peering over the stall, and Ava pushed between them to look too.

"Oh my gosh," she breathed, pressing her hands to her mouth. "What's he doing here? Hello? Who are you? How did you get here?"

"He's tied up," Levi said, pulling the stall door

open, making both her and Ava step back. He moved into the stall, and Tulia joined him, crouching down to begin working on untying the rough bit of cloth that was gagging Samuel. Levi was already working on the knot that was binding his feet together, while Ava just stared.

"I don't understand," she breathed. "This is your friend? Is this … is this some sort of game?"

Tulia was shaking and was trying to calm herself down enough that she could untie the knot, but finally she looked up at Ava. "I know it was you," she said. "I know you're the killer. You killed that poor man from the supermarket, and who knows how many other people along the East Coast. Did you know about this?" That last was directed to Levi, who was pale and looked utterly shocked as he tried to saw through the rope with his pocket knife without hurting Samuel.

"You think Ava…" He trailed off, looking back at the young woman, then over to Tulia. He shook his head. "No. No way. I've been working here nearly her entire life. I know her almost as well as if she was my own daughter. She wouldn't kill anyone. She didn't do this."

"I *know* it was her," Tulia said. "The RV—she has

the same RV as me. That's what she was bringing her mom out to see, wasn't it?"

"She doesn't have an RV," Levi said. "She drives a truck with an old trailer attached. The trailer's got a bed in the front compartment that she sleeps in so she can be near her horse."

"The RV, it's ... it's my mom's," Ava said, her voice quivering.

Tulia's eyes widened. Olivia? It wasn't as if she hadn't considered it, but why? It didn't make any sense.

Finally, she managed to loosen the gag's knot enough so she could untie it and take it off Samuel, and he sat up, shifting as the ropes around his ankles came free and Levi started cutting through the rope binding his wrists. "Thanks," he rasped. "I thought I was done for. She caught me by surprise —I saw the RV parked at a rest stop and tried to investigate, and she came up behind me and got me with a rock, or something. I was already tied up when I came to. I managed to get my phone out of my pocket, but she must have heard me trying to use it because she stopped the RV and took it away."

"Who did this?" Levi asked, looking Samuel up and down then looking around as if expecting the culprit to pop out of another stall. "I'm not going to believe you if you tell me it was Ava."

"It wasn't her," Samuel said, looking at the younger woman, who had her hands pressed to her lips and an expression of horror on her face. "No... It was her." Tulia followed his gaze, hearing the sound of a shotgun being racked. Olivia was standing in the middle of the barn behind her daughter, staring at them with a pale face and a grim expression.

"Ava, sweetie, go back in the house," she said.

"Mom, what's going on?" Ava asked, jumping and turning quickly, as if she hadn't known the older woman was there.

"Back in the house, now. I'll tell you about it later."

For a second, Tulia thought Ava was going to do it, but then the young woman straightened up, bracing herself. "No. I don't know what's going on, but I'm not going to leave. This man was tied up in our barn, and they're saying you had something to do with it. What's going on, Mom?"

"Sweetie," Olivia said. "I'll tell you everything, but you have to leave. You don't want to see this." Olivia eyed Levi, Tulia, and Samuel, and slowly raised the shotgun toward them.

"Mom!" Ava moved over, spreading her arms and

standing between her mother and the three of them. "What the heck are you doing? You're not going to *shoot* them. We've got to go to the police. They're saying you ... you're some sort of serial killer."

"Ava. Move."

They stood like that for what felt like a long time, though it must have only been a few moments before Ava moved. She didn't move out of the way, though. She stepped toward her mother. Tulia and Levi helped Samuel up, and he rubbed at the rope marks on his wrists. She had no idea how long he'd been tied up for, but it was hours, at least.

"I'm not getting out of the way," Ava said. "Tell me what's going on."

Olivia raised the gun sharply, and Ava flinched. It went off with a deafening bang, and all four of them jumped, but it was aimed at the wall above Ava's head, making woodchips rain down. Anger and frustration was evident on Olivia's face. "You want an explanation? How do you think it felt to watch you become the rodeo star I should have been? How do you think it feels to watch your daughter shoot right past your old level of fame and be more than you ever could have been? I love you, Ava, but I should have been the one touring the country. And I would've been, but I had to take time off to raise you. I'm happy for you, but you have no idea what it's like to watch someone else, someone you love, achieve everything you've ever wanted. Everything you could have been. My face should have been on billboards all over the state; instead, it's on one two-decade old billboard five miles from our house. I haven't even paid rent on it for years; it's been forgotten just like I have."

"So you kidnapped a man because you were jealous of me?" Ava asked. "That doesn't make any sense."

"You wouldn't understand," Olivia said. "Please, sweetie, just go inside."

"No. Tell me anyway, even if you think I won't get it. Mom, I need to know what's going on."

Ava's voice broke, and something in Olivia's expression softened. Tulia didn't dare to move, in case she drew the woman's attention back to them. "It started two years ago," Olivia said. She spoke hesitantly, but almost hopefully, as if she thought there might be a chance her daughter would understand after all. "It was when you went on your first tour down to Texas. We still had the old RV, and I was following along behind you while you took off in your truck and trailer. You were so happy, you never even noticed how much I was hurting. We were driving through some city or the other—I don't even remember where it was now—and I stopped to get some gas. This man came up and asked if I could give him a ride to the next town. I knew it was dangerous, but I agreed anyway. He was perfectly nice, and didn't say much, and before long, he had fallen asleep in the passenger seat right next to me. I don't know why the thought came to me, but I thought to myself, I could kill him now, and no one would ever know. The thought kept growing and growing as the miles went by, and finally, I pulled over. I didn't feel jealous or bitter anymore. I felt … alive. I took out my knife. He didn't even wake up until I'd already cut his throat. I didn't realize it would bleed so much—that was my biggest mistake. But it was such a thrill, Ava. You can't understand. I knew I couldn't stop with him. It was *my* secret, the thing that made *me* special. When I killed those men, I was the one who was powerful. The knowledge of what I had done, what I was continuing to do, kept me going while everyone was fawning over you. And then I just… I couldn't stop."

Ava's hands were pressed to her lips again, but finally she said, her voice shaking. "That… That was when you told me you cut your arm, wasn't it? And you convinced me to get the new RV instead of reupholster the old one, because your blood was all over it. But … it wasn't your blood, it was his. An innocent man's."

"I had to come up with some excuse," Olivia said. "But don't you see? It's better this way. This way I can follow you around the country, and I can help you out, and I can be so proud of my daughter, and I don't have to worry about those bitter feelings coming back because I have my own claim to fame, and it only grows every time someone finds another body. We're both famous now, sweetie. Both of us. Just like it should be."

"No wonder you refused to take that old billboard down. It was a last reminder of your glory days." Ava gave a bitter laugh. "You were so jealous of me, I should've seen it. I just—I don't understand, Mom. How could you do something like this?"

Her shoulders began to shake, and Olivia took a step forward, patting her daughter's arm. "This doesn't have to change anything, sweetie. I'm still the same woman you've always known. I love you. I was doing this so we would have a better relationship, don't you see? I didn't want to be jealous of you anymore. I just needed to feel special too."

Ava just cried harder, and Olivia gently moved her out of the way, then began to raise the shotgun again, pointing it directly at Tulia. Samuel pulled her back, stepping in front of her, but Tulia knew it wouldn't matter. If Olivia shot them, there would be nothing they could do to protect themselves. Levi was backed up against the corner of the stall, his hands raised as he stared at his boss like he didn't recognize her.

But Ava gathered herself enough to push the gun out of the way and step in front of her mother again. "Don't," she said, her voice strong beneath the tears. "Mom, if you do this, I won't ever forgive you. If you do this, I won't be your daughter anymore."

Olivia lowered the gun slightly. "Ava, sweetie, I have to. They're going to go to the police otherwise."

"And I'm going to go to the police either way," Ava said. "Are you going to shoot me?"

"Oh, sweetie, I'd never—"

"Then don't. Don't hurt them. The things you've done... It's too much for me to even comprehend right now. I just know if you do this, I'm going to walk away. I won't visit you in prison, I won't write you letters, I won't talk to your psychologist or read your apologies or try to understand it all. After what you told me, I don't know if I can ever forgive you or see you as anything but a monster, but I know for sure that if you kill these people in front of me, it's over. If you really love me, you won't do it."

Olivia looked the three of them over again, her gaze catching Tulia's for a second. She looked bleak. Tulia tensed, not sure which way this was going to go, but slowly, the shotgun lowered and then dropped to the floor. Behind Olivia, a horse blew out air in a snort.

"I'm sorry," Olivia said. "Ava, I'm so sorry."

She embraced her daughter, and Ava stood stiffly, not returning the hug but not pulling away either. Carefully, Samuel reached for the stall door, but Levi pushed past him, shoving out of the stall and running out of the barn. Tulia watched him run away, not able to blame him. She doubted any of this had been in his job description.

"The phone's inside," Ava said over her shoulder to Tulia and Samuel. "Call the police. I'll wait with her in here."

EPILOGUE

"So, what are you going to do after this?" Samuel asked. They were at the local police station—a tiny building, and one that would probably be telling the story of Olivia Adkins's arrest for years to come, if not decades—and had given their statements. It was the next morning, but Tulia didn't feel well rested. She and Samuel had parted ways the night before when he was taken to the hospital to be looked at for his head injury and dehydration. He seemed okay, which was one small blessing in this mess.

"Try to have a real vacation, I guess," she said. "Without two guys following me, and without hunting down any serial killers." She smiled, trying to lighten the mood, but wasn't sure if it worked. "How about you?"

"I should head home," he said. "I'm sure there's another case on my desk as we speak, and I want to make sure Marc is healing up as well as he says he is. But... I'm thinking of taking some time off first. This has been a heck of a case, and I'm not sure I have it in me to go back to work again right away."

"Well, I'm going to keep heading west," Tulia said. "I probably won't run into you again, but if I do, just come say hi, right? No more of this following me for miles in a black SUV and all this shady, secret-agent stuff."

He laughed. "All right, no more stalking—well, unless I get hired to do it." He grinned, obviously joking, but the words hit her harder than expected.

"Actually, can you tell me if someone tries to hire you to follow me?" she asked. "I almost forgot about it with everything that happened, but Marc said he talked to a PI who was looking for me. I think my ex hired him."

"Really?" He ran a hand through his hair. "Yeah. Wow. Sorry, bad joke I guess. I will definitely let you know if I hear anything about that. Like I said, though, I don't think I'll go back to work right away. I might take a road trip myself."

"Well, I hope it's more relaxing than mine has been. Stay in touch, all right? This is weird—I mean, we barely know each other, but you and Marc were following me for so long, then all of this happened. I'm almost going to miss you guys."

"I owe you more than I can say," Samuel said. "If you ever need anything, give me a call. Or call Marc, but since he's on the other side of the country right now, he might not be so helpful."

"I will, and that goes for you too, though maybe try not to get kidnapped by a serial killer again, all right? I really don't want to go through that again, ever."

He laughed. "I'll try, but no promises."

They gave each other a brief, slightly awkward hug, then let go and shook hands. Tulia watched as Samuel walked toward his rental vehicle. His black SUV had been left behind when he was kidnapped, and she supposed he would go to recover it soon. She felt strangely lonely as she watched him go, but a sharp whistle from inside the open windows of her RV reminded her she had her own companion waiting for her to rejoin him.

Going back into the RV, she shut the windows, kicked the AC up a notch, and took a deep breath. It was time to move on. She had caught a serial killer, saved a friend, and now, she had a trip to get back to. The West Coast was calling her name.

Made in the USA
Coppell, TX
03 October 2023

22364762R00063